CHOMPS
FOR BIGGER READERS!

Walter Wants to be a Werewolf!

Although Walter Grimm belonged to
an old and distinguished family
of werewolves, he was different.
While the rest of his family changed into
their wolfish form every time
there was a full moon,
Walter's skin only developed smooth
greeny-brown patches.

The family was worried, Walter was worried,
and so was his doctor, Dr. Van Fang…

MORE CHOMPS TO SINK YOUR TEETH INTO!

THE BOY WHO WOULD LIVE FOREVER
Moya Simons

STELLA BY THE SEA
Ruth Starke

THE TWILIGHT GHOST
Colin Thiele

Walter Wants to be a Werewolf!

Will Walter Grimm ever fit in?

Richard Harland

RUNNING PRESS
KIDS
PHILADELPHIA·LONDON

First published by Penguin Books Australia, 2003

Printed in China

9   8   7   6   5   4   3   2   1
Digit on the right indicates the number of this printing

Library of Congress Control Number: 2005935409

ISBN-13: 978-0-7624-2651-5
ISBN-10: 0-7624-2651-9

Original design by David Altheim and Susannah Low, Penguin Design Studio.
Additional design for this edition by Frances J. Soo Ping Chow

Typography: ITC Berkeley, MetaPlus, and New Century Schoolbook

This book may be ordered by mail from the publisher.
Please include $2.50 for postage and handling.
But try your bookstore first!

This edition published by Running Press Kids, an imprint of
Running Press Book Publishers
125 South Twenty-Second Street
Philadelphia, Pennsylvania 19103-4399

Visit us on the web!
www.runningpress.com

Ages 8–12
Grades 3–6

For Chris and Michelle

Walter Grimm belonged to an old and distinguished family of werewolves. Walter's mom and
dad changed into their wolfish form every time
there was a full moon. Walter's older brother
Stefan had made his first change when he was
twelve, his sister Sigrid had made her first change
when she was only eleven. They'd both been
grown-up werewolves for years. But Walter had
reached the age of thirteen and he still hadn't
made his first change.

"He's a late developer," said his mom. "Like my

1

cousin Agatha. Look how hairy she turned out in the end."

They waited until the next full moon after Walter's thirteenth birthday. Then they took him out on to the back lawn in the middle of the night. As soon as they were under the moonlight, the others all changed into wolves. Big beautiful wolves with thick grey coats, bushy tails, and lollopy red tongues. They shrugged off their human clothes and padded around on the grass. But not Walter.

"Take off your pajama top," said Mom.

Her voice was deep and husky, and her tongue got in the way of the words. A stranger would probably have heard it as a bark. Werewolves don't usually speak much when they're in their wolfish form.

Walter took off his pajama top and stood with his bare chest and shoulders in the silvery light. He looked up at the moon and felt very strange inside. He was sure that something was going to happen. This was it!

He waited and waited. But nothing.

"Think of running on all fours," said Dad. "Think of growling and howling. Think of peeing on trees."

Walter tried. He closed his eyes and pictured a huge wolf—not grey, but white as snow. He wanted to be that wolf. Sharp teeth, long muzzle, pointy ears. Power and speed, pulsing blood, and panting breath . . .

Harder and harder he concentrated. Had he done it?

He opened his eyes. The others were all staring at him.

"Yurrrk!" gasped Sigrid.

"Gharrr!" snorted Stefan.

Their jaws were wide open in shock and horror.

"What *is* he?" demanded Dad.

Walter looked down. There were patches where the skin had changed on his chest and forearms. But not hairy—smooth! Not white—but a sort of greeny-brown!

He touched the patches with trembling hands.

"They're hard," he said. "Hard and cold. I'm starting to feel stiff all over."

Mom burst into tears. At least, it would have been tears if she'd been in her human form. In her wolfish form, it was more like a kind of whimpering.

They hurried him back inside the house and took him up to his bedroom. They lowered the blinds, pulled the curtains, and blocked out every glimmer of moonlight.

Still they hadn't finished. They made him get into bed and covered him up with blankets. Blankets on top of blankets on top of blankets. It was like being in a cave with a tiny breathing hole.

4

Away from the full moon, the stiffness began to disappear. After another hour or so, the patches were gone too.

He got up to tell everyone he was back to normal. But his bedroom door had been locked.

The very next day, Mom and Dad went with Walter to see a special doctor in the city. Dr. Van Fang was an old vampire who was also an expert on all diseases of the body and mind. He wore little plastic safety caps on his two long teeth at the sides.

"And vot is zer trouble, Mrs. Grimm?"

Mom told the story of what had happened last night.

"Za-hah! I must examine zer patient."

Dr. Van Fang took Walter's temperature, looked

down his throat and tapped on his back and chest. He brought out a magnifying glass and examined the places where the patches had been. He had stinky bad breath.

"Zo . . . zo . . . zo," he muttered. "Not good, not good at all."

"What is it, doctor?" asked Dad.

"I cannot say. Zis is a new kind of case."

"It won't stop him turning into a proper werewolf, will it?"

Dr. Van Fang shook his head gloomily. "He will never become a proper werewolf. He does not have zer wolf-essence in him. Zer physical structure is all wrong. How long has he been zis way?"

"What way?" Mom demanded.

She was trying to defend him, but Walter knew what the doctor meant. Everyone else in the Grimm family had deep amber eyes and thick eyebrows. Even in their human form, they had a wolfish look. They were all long and lean and rangy. But Walter was, well . . . chunky. Big for his age, and solid with it.

"We thought it was just a phase," said Dad miserably. "We thought he'd grow out of it."

Dr. Van Fang paced up and down on the carpet. "And how is zer boy's coordination?"

"He's, er, not too bad . . ." Mom began.

"Yes, I am," Walter interrupted. "I'm hopeless. I've never been any good at any sports."

It was one of his greatest disappointments. He had always wanted to be like Sigrid and Stefan. Even in their human form, werewolves could run faster, spring higher and move better than ordinary human beings. Between them, Sigrid and Stefan held every athletics record at Brindaby High School. They were the best in every sport except swimming.

Dr. Van Fang sighed and sent another smell of bad breath wafting through the air.

"I blame zis modern world," he said. "New problems, new diseases. Not like it was when I was young."

Walter knew that it was at least five hundred years since Dr. Van Fang had been young. But he said nothing.

Dr. Van Fang made him lie down on a couch. He asked him questions about his schoolwork, his dreams, his eating habits. What were his hobbies? What was his favorite music? What shows did he watch on TV?

Walter answered honestly, but his heart sank as Dr. Van Fang's face grew more and more stern. What was he saying that was wrong?

Finally the doctor turned to Mr. and Mrs. Grimm.

"As I suspected! Not enough Nature! Too

much concrete instead of grass. Too many closed rooms instead of fresh air. Too much playing of computer games, too much heavy metal music, too much riding in buses and cars."

"But ... but how else can you bring up a child nowadays?" Mom asked despairingly.

Dr. Van Fang shrugged. "In zis case, some crucial limit has been passed."

Dad ground his teeth. "So even if he alters his lifestyle from now on ... ?"

"It is too late. It will make no difference. You cannot cure zis disease. You can only prevent zer symptoms."

"By keeping him away from the full moon?"

"It must be avoided absolutely."

Mom sniffled and wiped her nose. She always had a cold nose.

"I can't believe it," said Dad. "How will we ever live this down?"

He paid Dr. Van Fang for the consultation. Walter followed Mom out of the room. Dr. Van Fang's fee was two bottles of red raspberry cordial.

chapter 3

That was the start of the worst period in Walter's life. The mere sight of him seemed to make his father depressed. His mother tried to be sympathetic, but her sympathy only made him remember what he wanted to forget.

At school, nobody knew except Sigrid and Stefan. But he felt like a failure with everyone, even the ordinary kids who never guessed he was *supposed* to be a werewolf. He became more and more clumsy, more and more hopeless at sports. It was as though thinking about it made it worse.

After a while, he started to get teased for being so "uncool." Nobody would have dared tease him in the past, or they'd have had Sigrid and Stefan to deal with. But now Sigrid and Stefan acted as though he didn't exist.

His meanest enemy was a kid who was new to the school. Mardy Mingus had slicked-back hair and a thin sharp nose. His eyes darted around and spied into other people's business. He was always boasting about his family and how much money they had. They had moved from the city to a farm on the outskirts of Brindaby.

Why did he want to pick on Walter? Maybe it was because he wanted to show how mean and tough he was, so he selected someone he didn't expect to fight back.

One day he went too far.

It was the lunch break. When Walter looked around for a place to sit and eat, the benches were almost all taken. Except for one particular bench with only a single person on it.

Walter didn't care that the person was Mardy Mingus. He sat down on the other end of the bench, as far away from Mardy as possible. Mardy was talking to some classmates. They seemed to be sharing a private joke.

What Walter didn't know was that Mardy had secretly unfastened the bolts of the bench. When Walter sat down, it was only Mardy's weight at the other end that kept the seat in place.

Mardy waited until Walter had a spoonful of pudding to his mouth before he gave a whoop and jumped to his feet.

Suddenly, Walter's end of the seat dropped and he fell to the ground with a thump. The seat went cartwheeling through the air and whacked him across the top of the head. The pudding sploshed out all over his face.

Mardy and his friends were wetting themselves with laughter. They pointed and jeered.

Walter lumbered to his feet and ran at Mardy.

Mardy tried to dodge, but he was laughing too much. Walter grabbed him by the shoulders and pushed him backwards.

"Hey! Lemme go!"

Walter was clumsy but he was also big. He kept pushing Mardy all the way across the yard. Now everyone was watching.

Mardy tried to wriggle away, tripped and fell over on his back. Walter crashed on top of him.

Whummpf!

Mardy went red in the face. He couldn't breathe and he couldn't break free.

"Ow! Don't!" he gasped. "My chest!"

Still Walter pressed him flat to the ground. Mardy's face crinkled up and he let out a blubbering sound. He was really hurting.

Only then did Walter release him. He got up on to his knees, still panting, still dripping pudding. There was a circle of onlookers all around. The teacher on duty would arrive in a moment.

Mardy wiped at the snotty wetness on his cheeks and nose. His eyes were full of hatred.

"I'll get you for this," he muttered. "I'll tell my mom. Ma Mingus will see to you."

But even Mardy's friends were embarrassed by his whining wheezy voice. Walter had won a small victory.

Walter had less trouble at school after that. Yet he was more unhappy than ever at home, because now a special night of the full moon was approaching.

It was the time of year when the town of Brindaby became the werewolf capital of the state. Families were coming from hundreds of miles around to attend the Brindaby Werewolf Carnival. There would be celebrations and entertainment and athletic competitions. Sigrid and Stefan had entered the sprint races, the hurdles, the long jump, and the cross-country. Mom and Dad had high hopes for them.

Walter felt completely left out. He would have to stay at home, away from the moonlight. The family had decided on the excuses they would make to explain his absence. That was the only time he'd come into the conversation.

At last the great night arrived. Walter was put to bed early, and the blinds were pulled down, the curtains drawn. He could hear excited voices below in the kitchen as the family made their last-minute preparations.

His parents came to his bedroom. They were still in human form, but his father was already springing about on his toes. The canvas bags round their necks contained snacks and refreshments for the carnival.

"We're off now, Walter," said Mom. "The moon's just risen and it's a perfect cloudless sky."

They covered him with blankets to hide him away from the full moon. For a final layer, they unrolled a heavy old rug on top of the blankets.

"We won't lock the door," said Dad. "We know we can trust you, can't we?"

"Yeah," answered Walter. "Have a good night."

He had to force himself to say it. *He* was going to have the most miserable night. But it wasn't their fault he couldn't turn into a proper werewolf.

They switched off the light and went out. The bedroom was in total darkness.

Five minutes later, he heard Mom, Dad, Sigrid, and Stefan leave the house. They went out on the front lawn, letting the moonlight change them. One by one, they stopped talking and started yipping and howling.

Then they leaped down the drive and out through the front gate. Walter heard the gravel crunch under their paws. The carnival was being held in open country three miles away. Three miles was no distance at all to a fast, powerful werewolf.

Walter lay under the blankets, remembering previous carnivals. He'd been able to attend when he was just the same as other kids who hadn't yet had their first change. He remembered the excitement, the cheering, the games. All gone, all ended forever! He could never risk growing those strange hard patches again.

The thoughts kept churning over in his mind for what seemed like hours. He was too unhappy to sleep.

Then he heard voices.

His family? Coming back already? But these were more like ordinary human voices.

Where? He couldn't be sure through the layers of blankets. Yet they sounded much closer than the street. In the front garden?

He wriggled his head out into the open air. Again he listened. The voices had fallen silent.

He kept very still. His heart was beating fast, the blood was pounding in his ears. Perhaps he'd imagined it?

He wanted to peep out through the window. But there was a problem. If he exposed himself to the moonlight...

What was that?

He listened in a new direction. The sound had come from downstairs. A creak? There it was again!

He *had* to find out! He threw back the blankets and got up in his pajamas. He checked for hard patches on his chest and forearms. No, nothing growing there yet.

Very quietly, he opened the door and stuck his head out into the corridor. He was scared, but he wouldn't let himself panic. Even if he wasn't a proper werewolf, he was still a Grimm. He had to live up to the family name.

He could see light shifting on the walls at the end of the corridor. He tiptoed along to the top of the stairs and leaned over the banister. Flashlights were moving below in the hall. Burglars!

There were four of them. They wore black tracksuits and black sneakers. Knitted woollen ski masks covered their heads, with holes for the eyes, mouth, and ears.

They were whispering together.

"Seems nobody's home."

"So easy!"

"No alarm system!"

"No dogs!"

The voices belonged to two men, an older woman, and a young boy. The man who mentioned the alarm system was built like a gorilla and spoke as though his nose was blocked. The man who mentioned the dogs wore a headband over his ski mask like an expert in martial arts.

"Okay, let's move it." The older woman snapped out orders. She turned to gorilla-man and martial-arts-man. "You two go and check that there's nobody upstairs. We'll start collecting the stuff down here."

"What if we find someone?" asked martial-arts-man. "Can I karate-chop them?"

"Just tie 'em up. You know what to do."

"Why can't we do the collecting?" grumbled gorilla-man. "Why do we always have to do the tying up?"

"You wouldn't know what stuff to collect," said the boy scornfully.

"Yes, I would. Money for a start. And . . . and valuables."

"What sort of valuables?"

"Valuable valuables."

"Enough." The woman silenced them. "I told you what to do. Now do it."

As the two men turned towards the stairs, Walter stepped back out of sight.

Where to hide? There was only the bathroom or the four bedrooms. Already the men were climbing the stairs.

Walter slipped into the bathroom and closed the door. But wouldn't they check inside every room? He stood flat against the wall in the corner behind the door.

He heard footsteps stop on the other side of the door. The handle turned and the door swung open. Slowly, slowly, wider and wider. Walter held his breath. If it opened any more, it would bump against his feet!

It stopped swinging just in time. Gorilla-man raised his flashlight and came forward into the room. He directed the beam all around. But he didn't think to look behind the door. He wasn't expecting to find anyone in a bathroom in the middle of the night.

He grunted to himself and went out.

Walter discovered what it was like to breathe again. He heard the two men checking inside other doors along the corridor.

After a while, he emerged from his hiding place and peeked out. The corridor was empty. At that moment, the two men had both gone into different bedrooms.

He didn't stop to think. Taking four swift silent paces along to the top of the stairs, he began to descend in the darkness.

If the woman or boy had stayed in the hall, he'd have been caught for sure. But they'd gone into the living room. The light was switched on and there were rustling clinking sounds. Walter guessed they were busy burgling.

He paused at the bottom of the stairs. What next?

chapter 5

His first thought was to escape straight out through the front door. Then he had a better, braver idea. There was no one in the kitchen. If he could get to the phone in the kitchen, he could call his family. Even in wolfish form, Dad carried the cell phone everywhere.

Walter nodded to himself. Yes, he'd call his family to come back at once. These burglars would wish they'd chosen someone else's house to rob!

His bare feet made no noise on the floor as he

crept across the hall and past the living room. The living room door was ajar, but nobody saw him go by.

He came to the kitchen at the back of the house, slipped in, and closed the door behind him. The room was in darkness.

He edged forward, finding his way by touch and memory. When he came to the kitchen counter, he felt for the phone on the wall. He unhooked the handset and punched in the number of the cell phone.

Brr... brr... brr... brr...

"Hello? Yes? Grimm here."

"Dad, it's me." Walter spoke very close to the mouthpiece. "You have to come back. We've got burglars in the house."

"What? Is that Walter?"

There were background noises at the other end of the line. It sounded like cheering and applause.

Walter whispered a little louder. "Burglars in the house, Dad!"

He didn't hear the reply. Suddenly gorilla-man and martial-arts-man were talking in the hall. They must have finished checking the bedrooms and come downstairs again.

"Hurry, Dad!"

Walter hung the handset back up on the wall. But he wasn't careful enough. His pajama sleeve caught on something and knocked it over.

It sounded like the glass coffee jar. It toppled and rolled along the formica top. If it crashed to the floor . . .

He swept out an arm and grabbed it just in time.

But even as he saved the coffee jar, he knocked over something else, something metal. It fell and hit the tiles with a resounding clatter.

Walter froze. If only they hadn't heard! He willed them not to hear.

There was a rush of footsteps and the door burst open. The beam of a flashlight shone full in his eyes. He was dazzled and blinded.

Then the light switch clicked and the kitchen was flooded with light.

Gorilla-man and martial-arts-man stood in the doorway. The old woman and boy came up behind them.

"Gettim!" ordered the old woman.

Gorilla-man charged forward, followed by martial-arts-man. Walter drew back his arm and hurled the coffee jar with all his might.

Perfect aim! The jar struck gorilla-man across the bridge of the nose!

Gorilla-man clutched at his nose, staggered, and went down. Martial-arts-man ran into him and went down too.

Walter spun on his heel and made for the back door.

He was nearly there when the boy sent the plastic kitchen trash can skidding across the tiles. It smashed into Walter's legs and knocked him sprawling to the floor.

Still he hauled himself forward the last yard. On all fours, he reached up for the key and unlocked the door. Seizing hold of the knob, he turned it and pulled the door open.

A pair of hands fastened around his ankles. Huge powerful hands! Gorilla-man had crawled across the floor after him.

Walter struggled and kicked in vain. Gorilla-man grunted and tightened his grip. Walter was dragged slowly backwards over the tiles.

In the next moment, the old woman appeared in front of the door. She slammed it shut. She raised her flashlight to hit him over the head.

Walter stopped struggling.

The old woman grinned. Her teeth showed

crooked and yellow in the mouth-hole of her ski mask.

"Well, well, well," she said. "What have we got here?"

The boy wanted to interrogate him. Martial-arts-man wanted to karate-chop him. But the old woman shook her head.

"Nothing's changed. We stick to our plans. Tie him up."

Martial-arts-man and gorilla-man produced lengths of rope from their tracksuit pockets. They turned Walter over on his front. With one length of rope, they bound his hands behind his back.

"Make the proper knot," said the old woman. "A Triple Burglar's Bowline, like I taught you."

They bound a second length of rope around Walter's ankles. Gorilla-man seemed to enjoy tightening the rope until it hurt. He was still nursing a grudge over his injured nose.

"Okay," said the old woman. "Next, another rope to join the other two."

They bent Walter into an S-shape and tied the rope around his hands to the rope around his ankles. He was completely helpless.

The old woman snapped her fingers. "Now, back to business. Remember, a good burglar always stays focused. Work before pleasure. The job comes first."

The burglars left Walter and went out into the hall. The old woman gave orders and they spread through the house. Walter heard them collecting all sorts of things. They seemed to be stacking them near the front door.

He could only hope that his family would get

back in time. How long would it take them, running at top speed? What if they didn't come back at all? Had Dad actually understood his message on the cell phone?

Five minutes passed, and still the burglars hadn't finished. The stack in the hall must be a mountain by now. They must be stripping the house!

Walter thought of his CDs, his books, his videos, his PlayStation. Would they take his sneakers? His clothes? His model planes? He was desperate.

Then he noticed something shiny under the side of the kitchen counter. It was a serrated steak-knife. Why was it on the floor? Of course, it must be the metal thing he'd knocked to the ground before. It had got him into trouble then, but it might help him now!

He had to cross the floor to get to it. He couldn't

use his arms and legs, they were too tightly tied. So he pushed with his toes and scrabbled with his fingers. He wriggled across the floor like a stranded fish.

It seemed to take forever, but at last he arrived. He propped himself up against the side of the counter and felt with his fingers behind his back. If he could only . . .

At that very moment, the boy and gorilla-man came marching into the kitchen.

Would they realize he'd changed position?

If they did, they didn't care. They ignored him completely. The boy opened drawers and looked inside cupboards.

"Take this," he said. "And this. And this. And this. And this."

The boy went off and left gorilla-man to do the hard work. Gorilla-man carried the microwave out into the hall, then the coffeemaker and blender, and all the other appliances. He packed cardboard boxes full of the best china cups and plates and cutlery. Back and forth he went between the kitchen and hall.

Walter was seething with frustration. He couldn't use the knife until he was on his own.

One by one, the items disappeared until there was nothing more to take. Walter breathed a sigh of relief. But now gorilla-man decided to have a snack. He opened the door of the fridge and looked inside.

"Hmm," he said to himself. "Cheese. Salami. Chicken. Not bad."

"You're not staying focused," said Walter loudly. "You're not a good burglar."

Gorilla-man made a snorting sound. "Shut it, you!"

"I'll call the old woman and tell her what you're doing. Shall I?"

Gorilla-man helped himself to a leg of cold chicken.

"She's not around," he mumbled through his food. "She's gone to fetch the truck."

"What truck?"

The answer came even as Walter asked the question. He heard the sound of a diesel engine and a truck rolling up the drive. It braked to a halt outside the front door.

Gorilla-man cursed. He bit off a last mouthful and put the half-eaten leg of chicken back in the fridge. Then he hurried out of the kitchen without another word.

The moment he was gone, Walter reached for the knife. He got his fingers round the handle and worked the blade into an upright position. He maneuvered it to make contact with the rope that joined his wrists and ankles.

Then he began to saw. He had to saw with tiny

movements, quarter of an inch this way and that.

He heard the burglars carrying load after load out through the front door. Thinking of his CDs, his PlayStation, and his model planes, he sawed faster and faster. If anyone came into the kitchen, they'd see what he was doing at once. But he didn't care about that any more.

Finally the rope parted. Now he could unbend from his S-shape. He used the knife to cut through the rope round his ankles. Then he wedged the knife between his feet and used it against the rope round his wrists. With the last stroke, the loops fell away. He flexed his fingers. Free at last!

He jumped up, turned, and headed for the back door. He didn't know how he was going to stop the burglars. But he'd find a way. It was up to him now!

The Grimms' house stood in the middle of a big garden like a park. Tall trees and clumps of bushes grew everywhere. As werewolves, they liked the feeling of having a forest of their own.

Walter ran round the side of the house. He ducked down below the level of the windows, out of sight. He'd totally forgotten about the light of the full moon.

At the corner of the house, he stopped and peered out. There was the truck, a monster of a truck! It was parked parallel to the front of the house, with its rear end facing towards him. The doors at the back had been thrown open and a metal ramp led up into the interior.

Already the interior was almost full. Walter could see cabinets and easy chairs and even rolled-up carpets. The two men and the boy carried the stolen goods up the ramp, while the old woman bustled around inside. She directed the arrangement of each new item as it arrived.

What could he do to stop them? As he stood there thinking, he became aware of a stiffness creeping up over his body. It was the kind of stiffness he'd experienced only once before.

The effect of the full moon! He was caught in a patch of moonlight! Silvery brightness fell over his back and shoulders!

He had to get out of the light. He tried to step backwards, away from the corner of the house, but his body wouldn't obey him. There was no

41

feeling in his arms and legs. The change must have gone much further this time.

He made a mighty effort to start himself moving. With a sudden jerk, he lurched forward, but not where he wanted to go at all! He was heading towards the front garden and the truck on the drive.

He sent frantic messages to his muscles. Finally one got through, and he slewed round and went off in a new direction. Over a flower bed and in among the trees. A massive trunk loomed up straight ahead. He couldn't stop.

Kerthubb!

With a dull thud, he crashed into it and spun away. Strangely, he wasn't hurt at all. There was only a jarring vibration through his body.

Now he was heading in a different direction. He plowed into a clump of bushes. Tangled stems and leaves couldn't halt him. But right in the middle of the bushes was another tree trunk.

Kerthub-b-b-b!

This time he came to a stop. He was stunned and dazed, as though he'd been hit on the head. He felt heavy and solid like a big lump of metal. For a moment, he seemed to have lost his sight.

He hadn't lost his hearing, though. He heard a shout from the old woman in the back of the truck.

"Hey? What was that?"

"I heard it too!" came the blocked-nose voice of gorilla-man. "Over there!"

"Let's see."

Footsteps came stamping across the drive, approaching the trees and bushes. Walter suddenly recovered his sight.

But it was different from his usual sight. It was like looking out from a tunnel: a small circle of clear vision surrounded by darkness. He stared through the leaves and saw the truck parked in front of the house. Every detail appeared close up, as if viewed in a telescope.

He couldn't see the burglars, though. They were already pushing into the bushes, rustling towards him. Then the rustling stopped.

Someone hissed a warning. In the silence, Walter could hear a soft crunching on the gravel of the drive. A leaping, padding sound. Could it be?

He seemed unable to swivel his eyes, but he could turn his whole head—if it was a head. Approaching along the drive were four great wolves with long jaws and deadly teeth. His heart filled with pride.

The Grimm family had returned!

chapter 8

They were panting from their three-mile run. They seemed fascinated by the truck parked in front of the house.

Walter wanted to call out and tell them where the burglars were. But somehow his throat wouldn't work. He couldn't make a sound.

The four wolves circled around the truck. Seeing the open doors and the ramp at the back, they padded up for a look.

"Rrrrrrrr!" Stefan glared and bristled. "That's my bookcase in there!"

To anyone else, it would have sounded like a deep low growl. But Walter could understand the words.

"And my bedside table!" snarled Sigrid.

They were enraged. They all sprang up into the interior of the truck and stood on the pile of stolen goods. They began digging with their paws and dragging things out with their teeth.

Walter was amazed that his family could be so easily distracted. They ought to be sniffing out the burglars. Recovering the stolen goods could wait.

"Here's our TV!"

"My jewelery box!"

"The living room heater!"

"My magazine collection!"

"Rrrrrrrrrrrrrrrrr-owff!"

Walter was in despair. He could hear the burglars whispering and making plans. Then they slipped off in the shadows.

When he saw them again, they had detoured around to approach the truck from the side. They tiptoed silently across the gravel and came up behind the open doors.

The Grimm family noticed nothing. Dad had just discovered his exercise bike and lifted his head, howling for vengeance.

Again Walter tried to call out. This time he managed to produce a small scratchy sound, very different from his ordinary voice. But it was too quiet for anyone to hear.

"Now!" shouted the old woman.

The burglars launched into action. Martial-arts-man and gorilla-man leapt for the ramp and flung it up inside the truck. The old woman and the boy leapt for the doors and swung them shut. There was a loud double clang.

"Lock!" shouted the old woman.

Gorilla-man reached for the lever that locked the bolts on the left-hand door. Martial-arts-man did the same for the right-hand door. The bolts slotted home, top and bottom.

Yips and yaps of surprise came from inside the truck.

Walter was stunned. His great family of were-wolves—the noble and distinguished Grimms—were trapped like a litter of puppies!

The old woman dusted her hands. "So much for that!"

Martial-arts-man whistled. "I never saw guard dogs as big as that before."

Inside the truck, Mom, Dad, Sigrid, and Stefan went berserk. They barked and snarled and bayed—so furiously that even Walter couldn't make out any words. They began hurling themselves against the sides of the truck. The panels boomed and even bulged a little. But the werewolves had no chance of breaking out through solid steel.

The boy laughed. "Dumb as well as big!"

Martial-arts-man turned to the old woman. "What do we do now?"

"We get out of here."

"What about the dogs?"

"We take 'em with us. We'll get rid of 'em later."

She turned and headed towards the cabin of the truck. The other three followed. The old woman pulled off her ski mask as she went. She had iron-grey hair drawn back in a bun.

When she climbed up into the cabin, Walter got a look at her face. Her skin was like old tanned leather, her mouth was a mean hard line.

Gorilla-man and martial-arts-man pulled off their ski masks too. Gorilla-man had a fleshy face with small piggy eyes, and martial-arts-man had a shaved skull and shiny studs through his nose and eyebrows. Martial-arts-man put his headband back on around his head.

They climbed up and closed the cabin door behind them. The old woman took the driver's wheel. She started the engine and the truck set off. It turned in a circle on the front lawn, then back on to the drive.

The boy was sitting against the passenger-side window. He hadn't pulled off his ski mask yet. But now he did. Thin sharp nose and slicked-back hair.

Walter stared at the familiar face. It was the face of his greatest enemy. Mardy Mingus!

chapter 9

Walter watched through the leaves as the truck sped off down the drive, carrying the helpless Grimms. What did Ma Mingus mean about *getting rid* of them?

He had to rescue his family. He knew where the Minguses lived. If he could move, he could follow them.

But could he move?

He checked himself over. He was sure his dimensions had changed. But he couldn't tilt his head to look at himself. His body felt hardened and stretched out. He had a hollow sensation like empty space somewhere inside him. And a distinctive smell that definitely wasn't human.

What about his heartbeat? He didn't seem to have one. But one part of his body was warmer than the rest. He concentrated on it and felt it move. He made it throb faster, then slower, then faster again. Good! That was something under his control.

He gritted his teeth—though he wasn't sure if he still had any teeth—and willed himself forward.

Once again, there was a sudden lurch. With a rumbling rattling sound, he battered his way out from the clump of bushes. Twigs snapped, leaves swished, stems cracked.

He veered to the left and avoided one tree. Then almost blundered into another. His normal clumsiness was nothing compared to this. He felt as though he was wrongly wired up.

He came out in the open under the moonlight. The warm part of his body throbbed faster and faster. He was heading straight towards the side of the house. About to crash into solid bricks and plaster—

Skreee-kreee-krung-g-g!

With a screeching metal sound, he brought himself to a halt. Just in time, just in front of the wall. He was vibrating all over from the effort.

Then he saw the shadow cast by the moonlight on the wall. The moon was behind him, it was *his* shadow. It had to be. Yet his head was a wide sloping turret and he had no neck at all! Impossible!

It was all wrong—but in a strange way, it was also right. It was the kind of shape he'd been feeling inside. He could identify with that shape.

What he needed was a mirror. A little further along the side of the house was the living room window. Glass glittering in the moonlight.

He headed towards it. Thinking of himself in a new shape, it was easier to control his movements. He swivelled and advanced and pulled up beside the window. His reflection looked back at him.

He was broad and massive...

He was smooth and metallic...

He was painted khaki...

He had tracks instead of legs...

He had a long gun-barrel pointing out of his turret...

Yes, he was a tank!

He gazed and gazed in wonder. So this was it. He had changed not into a wolf but a tank. Suddenly everything made sense. He was a were-tank!

And he didn't mind at all. Who cared about bristling fur and a tail? Who cared about long jaws and a lollopy tongue? He liked himself exactly the way he was!

He moved back and forth in front of the window, looking at himself from different angles. He could move without even thinking about it now. He admired the tiny wheels inside his tracks, he admired his heavy armor plating, he admired the bits of equipment fastened to his hull and turret. He raised and lowered his gun-barrel triumphantly.

Then he turned his turret through one hundred and eighty degrees and faced towards the moonlight.

"Thank you, moon," he said.

The words came out in a crackly megaphone voice. His first words as a tank! He couldn't speak like a human being, but he could speak like a tank.

Then he remembered the rescue mission he had to perform. No more time to enjoy his new appearance. He swung towards the front garden.

He felt wired up correctly. His engine roared. With a smooth surge of power, he accelerated.

The Minguses might have managed to capture four werewolves, but they'd soon wish they'd never tangled with a were-tank!

chapter 10

The Mingus' farm was outside town on the road to Kendall. Walter rolled along at top speed. His tracks made a thunderous clanking noise on the roadway. Lights went on in houses as he passed.

The streets were almost empty. He met three cars going the other way. The drivers goggled through their windshields and nearly drove off the road.

The only people walking were two men and a woman on the corner of Burralong Street. They pointed in amazement.

"What's that?"

"A tank in Brindaby?"

"In the middle of the night?"

"Must be on army maneuvers."

"But in *Brindaby?*"

Walter didn't bother to explain. If they were surprised at the sight of a tank, they'd be even more surprised at a tank that talked to them. He rumbled on, leaving them behind.

He followed the Kendall road for half a mile, then took the turn-off to the Mingus' property. He crossed a wooden bridge over a deep gully with a creek at the bottom. Ahead was the fence surrounding the property.

He slowed and approached quietly. The Minguses had put in a new fence, more than two yards high, with barbed wire at the top. The gate was locked with a chain and padlock. It was obvious they didn't want visitors.

Walter focused on the chain and padlock. He was learning how to alter his telescopic vision for different distances. He rolled up close and pushed the end of his gun-barrel through the loop of the chain.

It was like having an elephant's trunk. He rotated his head and swung the barrel sharply sideways. The chain was strong, but Walter was stronger. With a sudden *pwang!* the chain snapped and the padlock dropped off.

No one had heard, no one came to inspect. The farmhouse was set back fifty yards beyond the fence. Walter nudged open the gate and passed through.

Where was the truck? He could see several barns behind the house, along with wrecked cars and stacks of tires. The Minguses had turned the farm into a kind of junkyard.

He chugged forward, making a wide detour to

avoid the house. Now he could see the truck. It was parked behind the barns with its lights off.

He plowed across bare dirt, past trees, over bits of junk. He circled around and approached the truck from the back of the property.

He was relieved to hear faint sounds coming from inside. The Grimms were still there, still alive. He rolled up to the back doors, very quietly. But not so quiet that a wolf couldn't hear.

"What's that?" Dad growled.

"Sounds like a machine," answered Mom.

"They're coming for us," said Sigrid in a whine.

"They're going to feed us into a machine," grizzled Stefan.

Walter spoke in his megaphone voice. "Be brave! I'm here to rescue you."

They pressed their snouts against the crack between the doors, sniffing and snuffling.

"Who is it?"

"Me."

"Who's me?"

"Walter."

"It can't be."

"It is."

There was a moment of silence. Then, "Why are you speaking in that funny voice?"

"You'll see. I'm going to open the doors now."

He raised his gun-barrel to the lever that locked the doors. It was a tricky job to prod at the right angle. The Grimms were pushing against the doors from inside.

Then suddenly the lever slid up and the left-hand door flew open. The Grimms burst forth in a whoosh of grey fur.

"*Yi! Yi! Yi! Yi!*"

They yipped and yelped when they landed on top of Walter's metal hull. They sprang down to the ground in a hurry.

"Hush!" said Walter sternly. "It's only me."

Mom blinked her yellow wolfish eyes. "Where? Where are you, Walter?"

"It's all me," said Walter. "The whole tank. I'm a were-tank."

It took them a while to believe it. Walter had to explain everything that had happened from the very beginning. Dad shook his head in amazement.

"I've never heard of such a thing. My son a were-tank!"

He sounded as though he didn't know whether to be pleased or horrified. But Mom rubbed her fur against Walter's tracks.

"You saved us, Walter. You're a wonderful were-tank!"

Sigrid interrupted. "What about the burglars? Where are they?"

Walter swung around to point at the house with his gun-barrel.

"There," he said. "Ma Mingus and the Mingus family."

Stefan ground his teeth. "They called us big dogs. They said they were going to get rid of us."

"Let's teach them a lesson," growled Sigrid.

They were ready to race off to the house immediately. But Walter halted them.

"Wait!" he ordered.

Sigrid and Stefan weren't used to being given orders by their younger brother. But they didn't know how to argue with something as big as a tank.

"You got yourselves captured last time," Walter reminded them. "Let's see what they're doing before we attack."

So they set off very cautiously. Mom and Dad leaped along beside Walter, while Sigrid and Stefan went on ahead.

They passed a barn, a pig pen, and an enormous brown pile of manure. Sigrid and Stefan peered inside the barn and ran back to report.

"It's packed to the roof!"

"With stolen goods!"

Dad looked at the other barns.

"They must be using the farm to store their loot," he said.

Walter concentrated on where he was going. By now he was incredibly skillful at every maneuver. He steered round a back garden shed and under a clothes line.

The house was made of weatherboard, raised off the ground on brick supports. The blinds had been drawn but the back door was open. Through the door came the sound of a TV.

Sigrid and Stefan crept up to the door and peered in through the insect screen. Stefan waggled his muzzle to show it was safe to approach.

Mom and Dad joined Sigrid and Stefan at the back door. Walter headed for the nearest window. Travelling at a snail's pace, he kept his engine to the lowest possible throb. He stopped, tracks almost touching the wall, and found a gap in the blinds to look through.

The Mingus family was in the kitchen, sitting round a table. Gorilla Mingus and Martial-Arts-Mingus had bottles of beer in their hands. They were trying to watch a program on TV. But Ma Mingus wouldn't let them.

"So think about it." She had a cigarette hanging out of the corner of her mouth. "I'll ask you again. What have we learned tonight?"

Gorilla Mingus tore himself away from the TV.

"Er . . . watch out for guard dogs?" he suggested.

"Tie better knots?" suggested Martial-Arts-Mingus.

"What we have learned is to *listen to your ma!*" Ma Mingus thumped the table with her fist. "What could have happened when the dogs turned up? Where would you be if I hadn't told you what to do?"

"Bitten all over," answered Mardy.

"Bitten all over," Ma Mingus agreed. "Bitten and bleeding. But Ma looked after you. Ma has the brains. Always remember it! Ma knows best."

"I've got brains too," said Mardy. "I selected the house and set up the robbery."

Gorilla Mingus snorted. "Only because you wanted to pay back that kid!"

"Yeah!" Martial-Arts-Mingus took a swig from his bottle of beer. "Only so's you could watch his videos and play his CDs. Only so's you could gloat."

"Nothing wrong with gloating." Ma Mingus came to Mardy's defence. "Gloating indicates a mean and nasty character. You all need to become more mean and nasty. Like your ma. You'll never be good burglars if you're not mean and—"

"What's that?" exclaimed Mardy suddenly.

Walter swung round towards the back door. Mom, Dad, Sigrid, and Stefan ducked their heads out of sight.

"What's what?"

"I thought I saw shadows outside."

"I can't see anything," said Ma Mingus.

Gorilla Mingus shrugged.

"When do we unload the loot?" he asked.

"We have to deal with the dogs first," said Martial-Arts-Mingus.

"How do we do that?"

They looked at Ma Mingus. She spat the cigarette from her mouth and trod it into the floor.

"A gas canister," she said. "We lob it into the back of the truck and wait till they're all unconscious."

"Whooee!" Martial-Arts-Mingus liked the idea. "Then we get rid of 'em!"

Ma Mingus turned to Mardy. "You know where we keep the gas canisters, Mardy. Go fetch one for your old ma."

Mardy wasn't listening. "There *is* someone out there," he insisted. "Watching us through the screen. I'm going to see."

He pushed back his chair and stood up, but he didn't reach the door.

Instead, Walter boomed out an order in his loudest megaphone voice. "*Attack*! *Attack*! *Attack*!"

chapter 12

Dad led the charge. He hurled himself at the screen door and burst clean through the mesh. Mom, Sigrid, and Stefan leapt through after him.

The Mingus' eyes popped almost out of their heads.

"It's—"

"It's—"

"It's—"

"Run!" shouted Ma Mingus, breaking the spell.

They jumped up and ran from the room. The Grimms chased after them, jaws wide and panting.

Walter powered up his engine and surged forward. He smashed through the window and the weatherboard wall. There was a tremendous crunching grinding sound. For a moment, everything was flying glass and chips of wood and plaster dust.

Because the house was raised off the ground, Walter didn't travel over the floor—but through it. He was like a ship plowing through ice. His tracks chewed into the floorboards and tossed them aside.

He followed the others across the kitchen. Too wide to fit in the doorway, he punched a hole through the interior wall.

Now he was in someone's bedroom. He arrived just in time to see a bushy grey tail disappearing through an open window. The Minguses must have escaped from the house with the Grimms in pursuit.

He plowed on, slow but irresistible. He steamrollered a bed, demolished a chest of drawers, battered through another wall. More flying glass and chips of wood and plaster dust.

Rafters collapsed behind him and he was out in the open again. If he'd turned to look, he'd have seen the roof of the house starting to cave in. But he didn't turn to look. He was only interested in catching the Minguses.

Where were they? He swivelled towards a sound of barking. The Grimms were chasing two of the Minguses around the mound of manure.

Walter trundled forward at top speed. Bits of wood and plaster fell from him as he moved.

The two Minguses were Gorilla Mingus and Martial-Arts-Mingus. They ran in circles round and round the manure, with the Grimms racing after them.

"Split up!" yelled Walter.

The Grimms heard. They came at the Minguses from both sides at once. The Minguses made a dash for the nearest tree.

The Grimms weren't quite fast enough to cut them off. Sigrid got in a nip on Gorilla Mingus' ankle, but he tore free and left her with a triangle of tracksuit in her teeth. The two burglars climbed up the tree and vanished into the topmost branches.

The Grimms danced around the tree in a fury. They snarled and sprang and snapped in the air. But they couldn't climb the tree or reach with their jaws.

Walter calmed them down. "I can deal with this," he said.

He lined himself up ten yards from the tree. Then he accelerated and charged. He butted the trunk with his armor-plated front.

Thunk!

The tree shuddered. Half of its leaves dropped off. Gorilla Mingus and Martial-Arts-Mingus wailed in fright. But they managed to cling on. Walter reversed, then charged again.

Thunnnkkk!

He slammed into the trunk so hard that every branch shook back and forth. The rest of the leaves dropped off—and so did the two Minguses.

Gorilla Mingus landed sprawling on the ground. Martial-Arts-Mingus fell, doubled up, over Walter's gun-barrel. His legs hung down on one side, his head and arms on the other.

"Ummmmph!" he gasped.

The Grimms pulled back their ears and howled in triumph.

"Now we'll bite them!" cried Stefan.

But Walter had a better idea. He focused into the distance and took aim. He swung his turret and whirled his gun-barrel. Martial-Arts-Mingus went flying through the air.

He came down *splattt!* in the middle of the smelly brown manure.

Walter would have smiled if he'd had a mouth to smile with. Perfect aim, perfect coordination! He'd invented a new sport especially for tanks.

He powered forward and hooked the end of his barrel in under the other Mingus. A moving shot this time. In one smooth motion, he swung his barrel and lofted Gorilla Mingus high in the sky.

There was a second satisfying *splattt!* Gorilla Mingus landed right next to Martial-Arts-Mingus in the mound of manure.

"I shall call it tank-hockey," said Walter, more to himself than his family.

But at that moment, a pair of headlights snapped out across the ground. Then the roar of a truck engine coming to life.

It was Ma and Mardy Mingus. Walter had forgotten all about them. The truck moved off and headed towards the gate.

They were making their escape!

chapter 13

"Leave it to me!" Walter shouted to his family. "You keep a watch on these two!"

He rumbled off while the Grimms stayed behind. They were getting used to Walter taking command.

The truck had already passed the house, more than halfway to the gate. It was jolting over rough ground, but it would travel much faster when it came to the road. Walter would never be able to catch it then. He had to head it off before it reached the bridge.

He changed direction to take the shortest route. Instead of going round by the gate, he would follow the line of the gully.

He left the barns behind and raced towards the fence. He could see warning signs, red boxes, and special cables. It must be an electrified fence. But he didn't care. He charged into it at top speed.

There was a crackle of violet light and a shower of sparks!

Walter wasn't hurt at all. The electricity only gave him a tingle. He crashed through the fence and out on the other side.

In another moment, he arrived at the edge of the gully. The ground fell away in a steep slope. He chose his spot and went over the edge.

Down down down he plunged, at a dizzying angle. His tracks gripped the ground underneath. He hit the creek at the bottom with a great splash.

He levelled out and turned at once in the

direction of the bridge. The water wasn't deep. He roared along the bed of the creek, sending up sheets of spray on either side.

He came around a corner. Ahead was the bridge, its wooden beams spanning from bank to bank. Where was the truck?

Then he saw it. Ma and Mardy Mingus were travelling along at top speed. He had no chance of reaching the bridge first. What to do?

The answer came to him in the strangest possible way. It was a feeling he had never experienced before. Growing and growing, like a cylinder with a rounded tip. It was centered inside his gun-barrel. Another part of being a tank!

He aimed at the bridge. He would get only one chance. He had only one shell. The truck was almost there.

Krakkk!

A sharp bang and a recoil! A flare of fire and

clouds of smoke! The shell hit the bridge and blew it apart!

Walter was deafened by the bang, stunned by the recoil. But he kept moving. He arrived at the wreckage of the bridge.

Fragments of burning wood lay on the banks and in the water. It was impossible to see anything clearly in the smoke. But Walter could hear raised voices up above. Ma Mingus had braked to a halt just short of the explosion.

"What now? What now?" That was Mardy's voice.

"Shut up!" That was Ma's voice.

"You're supposed to always know best!"

"Shut *up!*"

They were still shouting at one another as Walter climbed the bank towards them. The burning wood didn't bother him at all. He tilted to an angle of forty-five degrees, then to more than forty-five degrees. With a final burst of power, he came over the top.

The truck was five yards away. Behind the windshield, Mardy's eyes grew suddenly as big as saucepan lids. Ma's face twisted in rage.

She stamped on the accelerator. She must have thought she could push Walter back into the gully. Truck and tank rammed into one another, head on.

There was a sound of screaming metal and roaring engines. Walter's tracks skidded, the truck's wheels spun round and round. They sprayed dirt and gouged troughs in the ground. They shoved at one another like two bulls with locked horns.

Walter stayed calm and determined. The truck was bigger, but he was stronger. He knew he could win. And he did.

The truck started to slide backwards.

Walter got a better grip with his tracks. Harder

and harder he pushed. He forced the truck back the way it had come. The din was earsplitting.

Baphooom!

With a mighty blast, the truck's engine blew up. The hood burst wide open and clouds of steam exploded from the radiator. Engine parts showered all around.

Walter didn't pause, not for a second. He kept the truck pinned in front of him. He could push faster now that the truck was without power. Ma Mingus wrestled uselessly with the steering wheel.

He knew exactly where he was going. He pushed the truck all the way back to the gate. Then through the gate, then around the side of the house.

The Grimms woofed congratulations as they saw him approach. They were still on guard around the mound of manure. Gorilla Mingus and Martial-Arts-Mingus were still in the middle of the manure.

Walter parked the truck next to the pile. He disengaged his armor-plated front from the truck's bumper.

"Get out!" he ordered in his megaphone voice.

Behind the windshield, Mardy's mouth gaped open like a goldfish in a bowl.

"It spoke to us, Ma!"

He sounded ready to burst into tears. Ma sounded ready to bite his head off.

"Don't be stupid! Tanks don't speak."

"It did! It did!"

"There's a driver inside."

"No, there isn't. It's the tank ... ow!"

Ma had clipped him over the ear.

Walter was losing patience. He raised his gun-barrel and pointed it through the windshield, straight at Ma's head.

"Get out!" he repeated.

Of course, it was only a threat. He couldn't have

done it even if he'd had a shell in his barrel. But Ma didn't know that. She was going cross-eyed, staring at the end of the barrel.

She slid sideways and out of the door on the driver's side. Mardy tumbled out after her.

They stood facing the pile of manure. Before they could think of escaping, the Grimms penned them in. Ma seethed and glowered at the four wolves.

"What do we do now?" Mardy was almost blubbering. "Tell me, Ma! I'm scared! I'm . . . ow!"

Ma had clipped him over the ear again.

"A fine son you turned out to be!" she hissed. "Crybaby!"

Walter pointed with his gun-barrel.

"Walk!" he commanded.

Ma and Mardy were trapped. There was only one way to go. Reluctantly, step by step, they advanced towards the mound of manure.

Walter encouraged them from behind, with

sweeps of his gun-barrel. He drove them relentlessly to the edge of the brown oozy pile.

"All the way!" he boomed. "Right into the middle!"

The two Minguses already in the manure watched Ma and Mardy approach. Gorilla Mingus and Martial-Arts-Mingus were unrecognizable. Only their heads and shoulders stuck out, coated with smelly blobs of sludge.

"Hi, Ma!" called Gorilla Mingus. "Is that you and Mardy?"

"Have you come to join us?" asked Martial-Arts-Mingus.

Ma didn't answer. She grimaced and closed her eyes. Then marched forward into the mound of manure. It came up to her knees, her waist, her chest.

Mardy followed, bawling at the top of his voice. Right into the middle.

chapter 14

Even in the manure, the Minguses kept arguing. Ma tried to clip everyone over the ear. The Grimm family stood round, watching the show.

Walter and Mom made preparations for towing the truck home. "It's the easiest way to take back all the things they stole," said Walter.

"Do you think you can pull it so far?" asked Mom.

"I know I can."

So Mom hunted around and found a length of cable. She looped one end around Walter's turret and the other around the front axle of the truck.

Then it was time to leave. Walter made a final speech to the Minguses.

"We're off home now," he told them. "When we get back, we'll phone the police and tell them about you. We'll tell them to come to your property and search in the barns for stolen goods. You'll never have time to hide it all."

Ma Mingus shook her fist at him. She, too, was coated in blobs of sludge.

"So you'd better start running as soon as we go," Walter concluded.

He swung around and set off, pulling the truck behind. Mom, Dad, Sigrid, and Stefan leaped alongside. When they looked back, they could see four brown figures crawling out of the manure.

"We should tell the police to search for stinky people!" cried Sigrid.

"And arrest anyone who smells like poo!" added Stefan.

They frisked around, barking with laughter. Sigrid suddenly leapt up onto Walter and stood balancing on top of his hull. Stefan leapt up and squatted beside her.

"Wait a minute!" warned Mom. "He's already pulling the truck! Don't give him more to carry!"

"It's okay." Walter wasn't worried. "I can give you all a ride. No problem."

Then Dad jumped up, followed by Mom. Walter towed the truck and carried his family through the streets of Brindaby.

"You're so strong, Walter," said Mom. "You must be much stronger than an ordinary tank."

"I wish I could be a were-tank," said Stefan.

"Even better than being a werewolf," agreed Sigrid.

The wolves lifted their heads to the full moon and howled as they rode along.

"Whoooo-eeeee-oooo!"

About Richard Harland

I decided I wanted to be a writer when I was about eleven, when my cousin and I sold adventure stories in the school yard at recess. (Not very profitable, but very very satisfying!) It took a long time for the dream to come true, but now I think it's the greatest job in the world to be a full-time writer.

My first published book was a comic horror novel, *The Vicar of Morbing Vyle*, my next three books were adult SF thrillers. Then I wrote three fantasy books for Young Adult readers: *Ferren and the Angel*, *Ferren and the White Doctor,* and *Ferren and the Invasion of Heaven*. The *Ferren* books are set in a future world where the Millennial War has been raging for a thousand years between the armies of Heaven and the armies of Earth!

I've always been fascinated by wolves, ever since hearing the story of Little Red Riding Hood. I wanted to write a comic novel where werewolves do the traditional thing of changing into four-legged animals. Then I thought, why only wolves? Isn't there anything else they might change into?

I like writing and reading fantasy and SF where something highly unlikely is made to seem completely realistic. The best part about writing *Walter Wants to be a Werewolf!* was having to imagine what it would be like to experience what Walter experiences, how it would actually feel to go through this amazing transformation.

You can find out more about Richard (and werewolves) on his website: www.richardharland.net

Or write to him at his e-mail address:
richard@richardharland.net